can   dy

ed   the sky
dy   was   can   dy
lu   mi   love is a place
nous   ed   through this pla
pinks   i   love move
ble   brightness o
spry   pinks
greens shy   lem
ons
greens   a world
cool
choco   lates

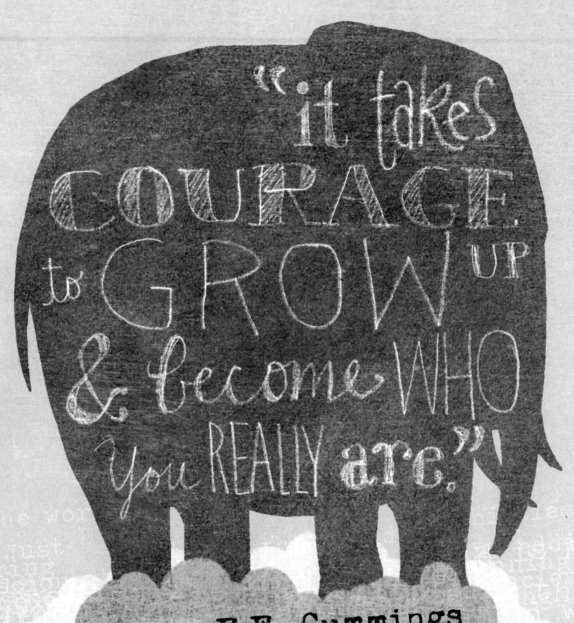

"it takes COURAGE to GROW up & become WHO you REALLY are."

E.E. Cummings

e.e. cummings

For Joseph Warford.   —M.B.

www.enchantedlionbooks.com

Text copyright © 2015 by Matthew Burgess
Illustrations copyright © 2015 by Kris Di Giacomo

First edition published by Enchanted Lion Books,
351 Van Brunt Street, Brooklyn, NY 11231

ISBN 978-1-59270-171-1

First edition 2015
Design and layout: Kris Di Giacomo
Printed in China by South China Printing Co.

10 9 8 7 6 5 4 3 2 1

enormous SMALLNESS

A Story of
E. E. Cummings

by
Matthew Burgess

illustrations by
Kris Di Giacomo

ENCHANTED LION BOOKS
NEW YORK

Inside an enormous city
in a house on a very small street,
there once lived a poet
I would like you to meet.

His name?

E. E. Cummings

Here is his window at 4 Patchin Place
in New York City.
Peek inside and you will see
the room where E. E. writes his poetry.

While sitting at his typewriter,
E. E. listens to the birds singing
outside his window:

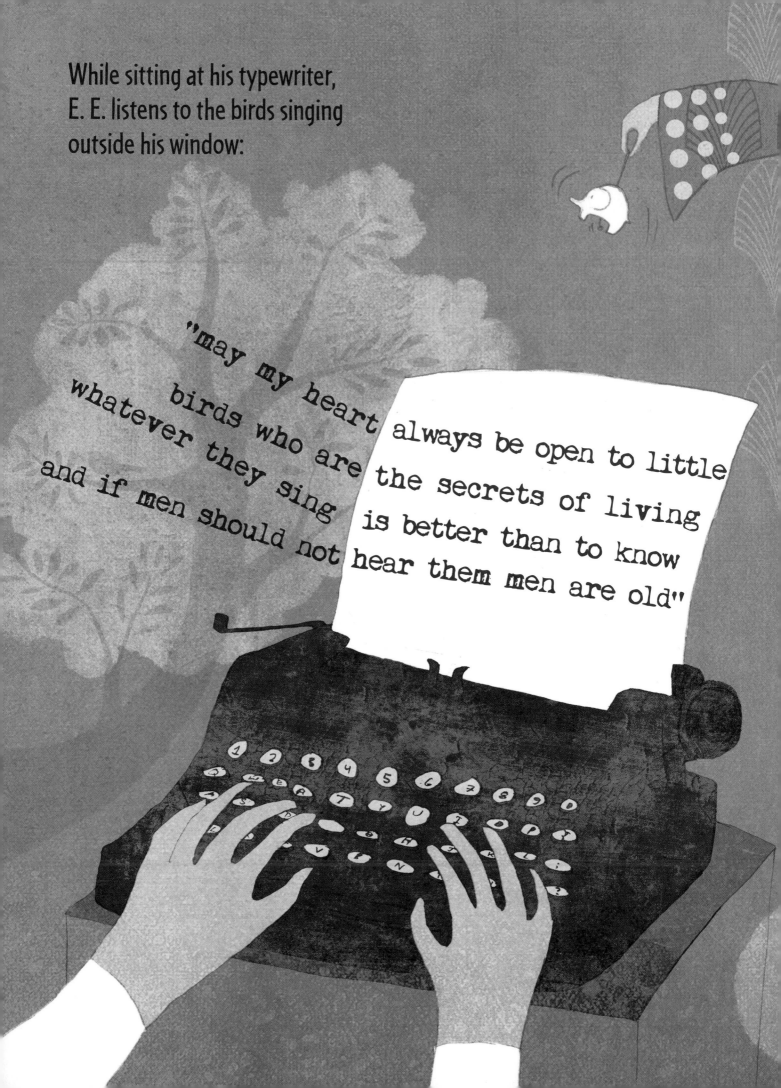

"may my heart always be open to little
birds who are the secrets of living
whatever they sing is better than to know
and if men should not hear them men are old"

In the room below his studio, a woman rings an elephant with a bell in its belly.

Time for tea!

She is Marion Moorehouse, a fashion model and photographer, and the love of E. E.'s life.

But how did he become a poet? And why is he called E. E.?

EDWARD ESTLIN CUMMINGS

was born on October 14, 1894.

His parents were
Edward and Rebecca Cummings,
and they lived in Cambridge, Massachusetts.

Estlin grew up in a lively house
at 104 Irving Street,

with his mother and father,
two grandmas, two aunts,
one rambunctious Uncle George,
his younger sister Elizabeth,
the handyman Sandy Hardy,
an Irish maid named Mary,
a dog, a cat, goldfish,
and some rabbits.

From his bedroom window,
Estlin could see enormous apple and cherry trees.

Looking out,
he watched the birds
        hop
from branch
            to branch
        and tree
to tree...

and his first poem
flew out of his mouth
when he was only three:

"Oh, my little birdie, Oh with his little toe, toe, toe!"

When Estlin said his poems aloud, his mom would write them down.
She made a little book and titled it, "Estlin's Original Poems."

When Estlin was six,
he wrote a poem about trees:

"Sunny in the morning,
Beautiful and Fair
Maple trees are happy
In the frosty air."

"Beautiful!"
his mom exclaimed.
"What else do you see?"

Estlin looked around
as if his eyes were on tiptoes
and when his heart jumped,
he said another poem.

"On the chair is sitting
Daddy with his book.
Took it from the bookcase
Beaming in his look."

Soon elephants started marching
into Estlin's poems and drawings.

Inspired by the circus and the zoo,
he pretended his father was an elephant
and he rode across the carpet on his back.

"Take me to the jungle, you enormous beast!"

Estlin would holler, and Mr. Cummings would **S T O M P** on hands and knees into an imaginary wilderness.

As Estlin grew, he drew many pictures from the great circus of his imagination.

But even more than drawing elephants, trees, and birds, Estlin LOVED WORDS.

What words say and how they sound and LOOK.

HE LOVED THE WAY THEY HUM, buzz, POP, and swish.

Estlin also liked to invent new words,
like this one:

"WHASH-HO ZEPHYR."

And he squished others
together, like this:

"beanhamegg."

Whether playing on the swings and monkey bars in the yard,
or leading his friends on adventures through the neighborhood,

Estlin knew how to make life fun.

Sometimes, when the wind was up, he and his sister Elizabeth
would climb the staircase to the copper roof of their house.
From their perch in the sky, he would fly his homemade kite

INTO THE WIND.

Sometimes they would
sit on the roof at night,
gazing up at the stars.

When school was out in June, Estlin and his family
went to Joy Farm in New Hampshire, where they spent

LONG
SUMMER
DAYS.

There, Estlin swam in the stream,
milked the cow, Buttercup-Daisy,
rode Jack the donkey, and wandered
with his dog Rex through fields and forests.

In the enchanted afternoons, Estlin wrote and drew
in the small cabin his father made for him
at the edge of the woods.

Back home on Irving Street,
in one particularly
enormous tree,
Estlin and his father
built a small house in the branches.
They even installed a stove
to keep him cozy on wintry days.

There, snug and warm,
Estlin and his friends would pop popcorn,
toast toast, and stir hot cocoa
on the little stove.

Estlin also liked being there alone.

Drawing pictures
and writing poems,
he would peer out
at the world above
and the world below.

When Estlin was eleven,
his favorite teacher, Miss Maria Baldwin,
noticed his wonderful way with words
and encouraged him.
From her, Estlin learned that

anything is possible,
as long as you are true to yourself
and never give up, even when the world
seems to say, stop!

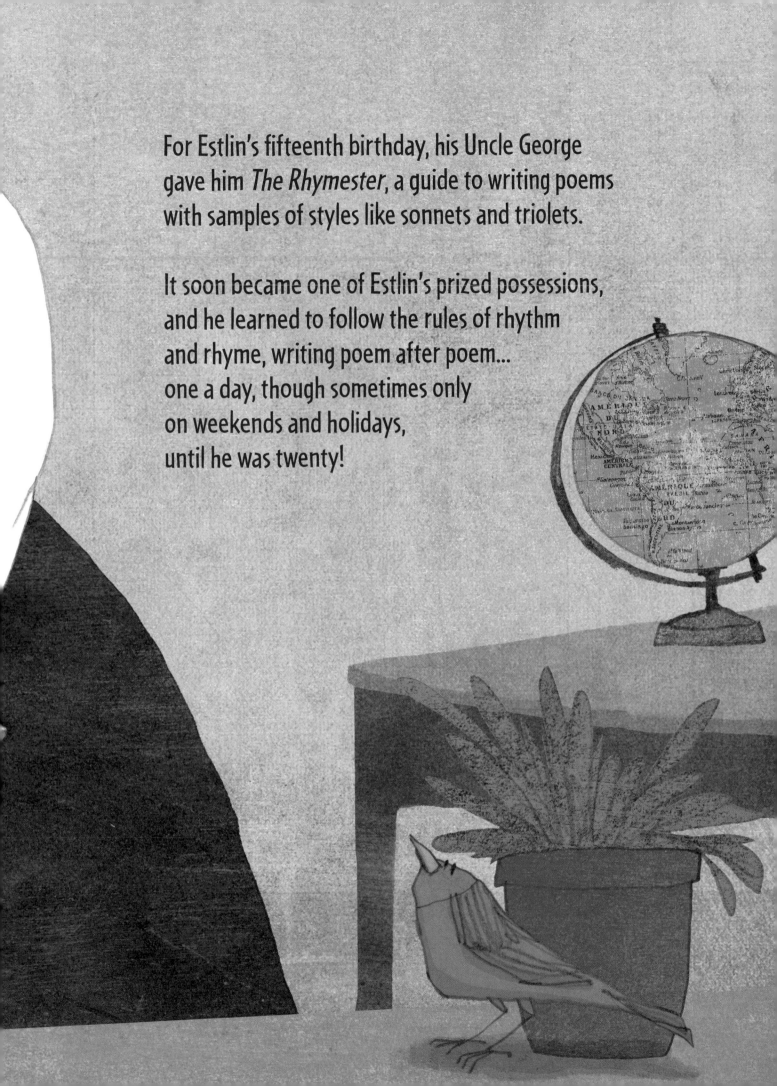

For Estlin's fifteenth birthday, his Uncle George gave him *The Rhymester*, a guide to writing poems with samples of styles like sonnets and triolets.

It soon became one of Estlin's prized possessions, and he learned to follow the rules of rhythm and rhyme, writing poem after poem... one a day, though sometimes only on weekends and holidays, until he was twenty!

A month before his seventeenth birthday,
Estlin began his freshman year
at Harvard College, just a few blocks away
from his home on Irving Street.

Estlin quickly made many new friends
and found professors who inspired him.
He also began publishing his poems
in the Harvard magazines.

In his senior year, Estlin moved from home
into his own dorm room in the center of campus.

He covered his walls with Krazy Kat comic strips,
and a parade of elephants marched across
his mantlepiece.

One day, Estlin read these words
by his favorite poet, John Keats:

"I am certain of nothing

but the holiness
                of the Heart's affections
and the truth of the Imagination."

Suddenly, deep within him,
a mysterious bird
began to sing.

Estlin knew it would
take courage to follow his heart,
but he was determined
to live the life he imagined.

At graduation,
Estlin electrified his audience
with a speech titled "The New Art."
He talked about Gertude Stein,
Paul Cezanne, and Igor Stravinsky,
artists who were challenging
the way we think and see.

In all of the arts,
people were in pursuit
of the new and Estlin
wanted to make his mark, too.

After graduation, Estlin returned to his old home on Irving Street. There, in his attic room, he experimented with his poetry.

But adventures awaited him, so when he had saved enough money, Estlin headed to New York City!

Filled with artists and poets, Greenwich Village was the place to be. He loved the city immediately:

"I also breathed...as if for the first time."

Estlin wandered the streets
with friends for hours on end.
Sometimes they'd stop at Khouri's
for shish kebab, or pop into bookshops
to browse for second-hand paperbacks.

He loved the city's

"IRRESISTIBLY STUPENDOUS NEWNESS."

But shortly after Estlin arrived in New York City, everything changed when the United States entered World War I.

It was April 6, 1917.

The very next day, Estlin volunteered to drive an ambulance in France.

Three weeks later, he boarded a ship to sail across the Atlantic.

Estlin's mother traveled to New York to send him off with a kiss, and his father sent a telegram to show he would be missed.

TELEGRAM

"AS I SAID IN ADVANCE I ENVY YOUR CHANCE OF BREAKING A LANCE FOR FREEDOM IN FRANCE BY DRIVING AND MENDING AN AMBULANCE BEST LOVE AND LUCK A SOLDIER EVER HAD, FROM BETSY, MOTHER, JANE, NANA AND DAD."

While awaiting his assignment
with the ambulance corps,
Estlin explored Paris
with his journal in hand.

Bowled over by the museums,
the ballet, and the colorful,
crowded streets,
Estlin drank in every detail.

After only a few weeks,
Estlin had to report for duty in the countryside,
but he would return to Paris many times
throughout his life.

While working for the ambulance corps,
Estlin was mistaken for a spy
and sent to prison.
He was released
a few months later.

When the war was over,
Estlin joined his family at Joy Farm,
where he wrote a book about
his experiences in the war,
called:

The
Enormous
Room

by
E. E.
Cummings

The book was published and praised!
Estlin was becoming E. E.!

A year later, his first book of poems
was published:

**Tulips
&
Chimneys**

Using a style all his own,
e. e. put lowercase letters where capitals normally go,
and his playful punctuation grabbed readers' attention.

His poems were alive with experimentation and surprise!

And because of his love for lowercase letters,
his name began to appear with two little e's (& a little c, too).

e. e. liked to break the rules of rhythm and rhyme and to make words

dance

ACROSS THE PAGE

in sur(priz)ing ways.

He wanted his reader's eyes to be on tiptoes too,
seeing and reading poetry (inaway)
that was new.

Some people criticized him for painting with words.
Others said his poems were

TOO STRANGE

too small.

But no matter what the world was giving or taking,
E. E. went right on dreaming and making.
For inside, he knew his poems were new and true.

```
love is a place

love is a place
& through this place of
love move
(with brightness of peace)
all places

yes is a world
& in this world of
yes live
(skillfully curled)
all worlds.
```

```
!
        o(rounD)moon,how
do
you(round
er
than round)float;
who
lly &(r0under than)
go
:ldenly(Round
est)
```

His poems were his way
of saying YES.

yes

YES to the heart
and the roundness of the moon,
to birds, elephants, trees,
and everything he loved.

YES to spring too,
which always brought him back
to childhood, when the first
sign of his favorite season
was the whistling arrival
of the balloon man.

in Just-
spring   when the world is mud-
luscious the little
lame balloonman

whistles   far   and wee

and eddieandbill come
running from marbles and
piracies and it's
spring

when the world is puddle-wonderful

the queer
old balloonman whistles
far   and   wee
and bettyandisbel come dancing

from hop-scotch and jump-rope and

it's
spring
and

          the

          goat-footed

balloonMan   whistles
far
and
wee

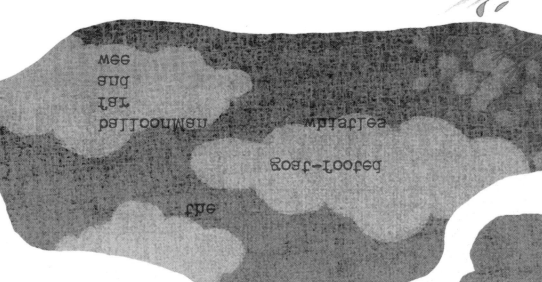

In time, more and more people came to see the beauty of E. E.'s poetry, and he became one of the most beloved poets in America.

"*Time for tea!*"

Marion rings the elephant bell. The table is set, the tea is ready.

E. E. lived at 4 Patchin Place for almost forty years.

When asked why, he would reply:

"because here's
friendly,
unscientific,
private,
human."

Like the tree house of his youth,
the "topfloorback" room was a small world
where E. E. could work and dream,
peering out at the world above
and the world below.

As an old man, Edward Estlin Cummings often remembered his childhood days in the lively house on Irving Street.

He could still see himself as a boy gazing out at the sunset...

...and like the little bird singing outside his window, E. E. sang.

And his song was his poem.

who are you,little i

(five or six years old)
peering from some high

window;at the gold

of November sunset

(and feeling:that if day
has to become night

this is a beautiful way)

chronology

1894   Edward Estlin Cummings is born in Cambridge, Massachusetts, on October 14th.

1897   Estlin, age three, begins saying his first poems to his mother, Rebecca,
who writes them down in a book titled, "Estlin's Original Poems."

1898   Edward Cummings purchases Joy Farm in New Hampshire. Estlin sees
this magical place, where he will spend his summers, for the first time in 1899.
Over time, Joy Farm will become the place where E. E. feels most alive and most connected
to the natural world.

1901   Estlin's sister, Elizabeth Frances Cummings, is born on April 29th.
Estlin fills a sketchbook with drawings of animals (especially elephants!)
and titles it "Animals at the Zoo."

1904   Estlin starts at the Agassiz Grammer School, where Miss Maria Baldwin is principal.
Baldwin, who Cummings later remembers as having "a delicious voice, charming manners,
and a deep understanding of children," was the first female African-American principal
in New England. In eighth grade (1905-06), she also becomes Estlin's teacher.

1907   Enters Cambridge Latin School, a prep school a few blocks from his house.

1910   First published poem appears in the **Cambridge Review**.
Estlin vows to write a poem a day!

1911-15   Harvard College. Estlin receives the distinction of *magna cum laude* in Literature,
and he delivers the commencement speech on "The New Art."

1916   Receives a masters degree from Harvard and begins painting in the Cubist style.

1917   Moves to New York City. On April 7th, he volunteers for the Ambulance Corps
and sails to France shortly thereafter.

1921-23   Lives off and on in Paris, spending time at Joy Farm as well.
In 1922, his memoir about his mistaken imprisonment for espionage,
The Enormous Room, is published to critical acclaim.

1923   His first book of poems, **Tulips and Chimneys**, is published.

1924   Moves into the third-floor studio at **4 Patchin Place**, his home for the rest of his life.

1925   Receives the **Dial Award** "for distinguished service to American letters."

1928   **Him**, a play in three acts, is produced at the Provincetown Playhouse.

1931   First major exhibit of paintings at the Painters and Sculptors Gallery.

1932   Meets **Marion Moorehouse**, the fashion model and photographer who will live with him as his wife for the rest of his life.

1938   Publication of **Collected Poems**.

1944-49 Several important exhibitions of E. E.'s paintings.

1950   Receives a distinguished fellowship from the **Academy of American Poets**.

1952-53 Delivers a series of lectures at Harvard, later published as **i: six nonlectures**.

1955   Begins a seven-year series of poetry readings at colleges and universities.

1959-62 Travels to Ireland, Sicily, Italy, and Greece.

1962   Suffers a stroke after chopping wood at Joy Farm. Dies on September 3.

poems

```
            the sky
            was      can dy
        lu               mi
            nous             ed
                             i
            ble
                spry  pinks
                shy           lem
            ons
                                greens
         cool
      choco              lates
            un                        der
      a   lo
          co
          mo              tive            s pout
                          ing
              vi
          o
                          lets
```

1916

love is a place

love is a place
& through this place of
love move
(with brightness of peace)
all places

yes is a world
& in this world of
yes live
(skillfully curled)
all worlds.

1935

```
            in Just-
spring          when the world is mud-
luscious the little
lame balloonman

whistles          far          and wee

and eddieandbill come
running from marbles and
piracies and it's
spring

when the world is puddle-wonderful

the queer
old balloonman whistles
far          and          wee
and bettyandisbel come dancing

from hop-scotch and jump-rope and

it's
spring
and

            the

                    goat-footed

balloonMan          whistles
far
and
wee
```

1923

```
                                who are you,little i

                                (five or six years old)
!                               peering from some high
o(rounD)moon,how
do
you(round                       window;at the gold
er
than round)float;
who                             of November sunset
lly &(rOunder than)
go                              (and feeling:that if day
:ldenly(Round                   has to become night
est)

                                this is a beautiful way)
```

1950

1963

author's note

In June 2007, I was invited to lead a "literary walk" of Greenwich Village. I had never given a tour before, so I took photographs of the buildings on the route and wrote notes on the backs for reference. A few days later, as I stood on the stoop of 4 Patchin Place, anxiously trying to remember snippets of E. E. Cummings' life story to share with the assembled group, the front door swung open. A woman and a boy emerged, and by a stroke of luck, the woman happened to be friends with someone in our group. We talked for a minute and then she asked, "Would you like to come in and see the place?"

Suddenly, the twelve of us were filing up the tilted narrow staircase and into the room where Cummings had worked for almost forty years. The windows opened to trees and birdsong, and the summer light filtered in. The room showed all the telltale signs of a young boy's bedroom, but it wasn't difficult to imagine E. E. Cummings writing and painting there. As the plaque beside the front door reminded us on our way in, Cummings was both a poet and a painter, and he once called himself "an author of pictures, a draughtsman of words."

Three years later, when my publisher, Claudia Zoe Bedrick, asked me if I would be interested in writing a picture book about E. E. Cummings, I remembered that day at Patchin Place, and I sensed another door opening. E. E. Cummings was one of the first poets to make a strong impression on me when I was a child, and the memory of visiting his home felt like an auspicious sign.

Plunging into research, I learned more about Cummings' magical childhood in Cambridge, Massachusetts. Elizabeth Cummings describes her brother's tree house in detail, and I was struck by the idea that E. E. had recreated his cherished childhood retreat in his small apartment on a half-hidden cul-de-sac in New York City. In a letter to a friend, Cummings wrote that 4 Patchin Place "meant Safety & Peace & the truth of Dreaming & the bliss of Work."

In many ways, Cummings was a champion of the small. He wrote about birds, grasshoppers, snowflakes, and other everyday pleasures. He frequently used lowercase letters, and he became famous for his use of the small "i." At a time when many of his contemporaries believed it was necessary to write a "long poem" to become established as a major poet, Cummings preferred smaller forms. Marianne Moore, the poet, called E. E. Cummings "a concentrate of titanic significance."

In 1952, Cummings received an invitation to deliver a series of lectures at Harvard. He accepted the offer, but with his characteristic mischievous wit, he titled them "i: six nonlectures," and he spoke at length about his parents, his childhood, and his development as a young poet. In the second nonlecture, titled "i & their son,"

Cummings recalls wandering through the woods near his home in Cambridge: "Here, as a very little child, I first encountered that mystery who is Nature; here my enormous smallness entered Her illimitable being…"

On reading this passage, I knew I had found the title of my version of E. E. Cummings' life—a story that seeks to capture the spirit of this imaginative boy who grew up to become one of our most distinctive and innovative poets.

acknowledgments

I am grateful to all of the biographers whose work has informed and guided my own retelling: Howard Norman's *The Magic-Maker*, Richard Kennedy's *Dreams in the Mirror*, Christopher Sawyer-Lauçanno's *E. E. Cummings: A Biography*, and Susan Cheever's *E. E. Cummings: A Life*. A special thank you to Catherine Reef, author of the young adult biography, *E. E. Cummings: A Poet's Life*, who replied to my inquiry with generosity and warm wishes. This book is the result of a close collaboration with Claudia Zoe Bedrick that began in January 2010. Claudia entrusted me with her idea, glimpsed the promise in my earliest drafts, and then worked shoulder-to-shoulder with me for four years to bring our book to fruition. Finally, I want to thank the artist Kris Di Giacomo for making our story so vivid and lively and lovely.

Just-
spring
ball

in
when the world is whistles
spring
luscious

in Just-
spring when the
luscious the little
luscious
lame bal

whistles
and
run

the sky
was   can   dy
lu   mi
nous   ed
i
ble
spry   pinks
shy   lem
ons